Ridicholas Nicholas

MORE ANIMAL POEMS

by J. Patrick Lewis   pictures by Victoria Chess

Dial Books for Young Readers New York

For my mother and the memory of my father
J.P.L.

To Isaac and Clea, with love
V.C.

Published by Dial Books for Young Readers
A Division of Penguin Books USA Inc.
375 Hudson Street
New York, New York 10014

Text copyright © 1995 by J. Patrick Lewis
Pictures copyright © 1995 by Victoria Chess
All rights reserved
Designed by Amelia Lau Carling
Printed in Hong Kong
First Edition
10 9 8 7 6 5 4 3 2 1

Library of Congress Cataloging in Publication Data
Lewis, J. Patrick. Ridicholas Nicholas: more animal poems/
by J. Patrick Lewis; pictures by Victoria Chess.   p. cm.
Summary: A collection of poems about animals, including the owl,
hippo, and hornet.
ISBN 0-8037-1327-4.—ISBN 0-8037-1328-2 (library)
1. Animals—Juvenile poetry. 2. Children's poetry, American.
[1. Animals—Poetry. 2. American poetry.] I. Chess, Victoria, ill. II. Title.
PS3562.E9465R5 1995   811′.54—dc20   91-44349   CIP   AC

The full-color artwork was prepared using pen and inks, dyes, colored
pencils, pastel pencils, and tempera paints. It was then color-separated
and reproduced as red, blue, yellow, and black halftones.

Contents

Oh, Where Are You Walking?

"Oh, where are you walking?"
  Said Speeder to Spider,
"The kitchen's a comfort,
  The basement is bare.
The chimney's a chamber
  Of charming enchantments,
So why do you weave
  Your silk on my stair?"

"I've located lodging,"
  Said Spider to Speeder,
"No cool corner cupboard,
  No warm windowpane.
I've sewn you a circle
  Inside of a shadow—
Then looped you a loop,
  And I looped it again."

5

Mrs. Hippos

You won't see any Mrs. Hip-
pos on the mighty Mississip,

And never on the Amazon
with silky French pajamazon.

Hippo ladies never rest
on top of old Mount Everest.

But look who's barging with a smile
single file up the Nile.

The Owl

The dark grows tall
  Above the trees.
She will not stir
  Unless she sees
A rabbit sigh.
  She will not soar
Until she hears
  A mouse's roar.

Tic-Tac-Toad

A Turkey and a Toad were playing
   Tic-tac-toe in Texas.
The Turkey said, "I'll take the O's,
   And you can have the X's."

But Armadillo scratched the game
   That Turtle cleaned and dusted,
Which made the Toad and Turkey tic-
   Tac-totally disgusted.

The Pretenders

The Raccoon
    wears a mask
    a robber's mask
    there's no mistaking

The Opossum
    up ahead
    who's nearly dead
    is merely faking

The Rabbit
    lying still
    is trying still
    to stop from shaking

The Fox
    at once a thief
    is twice a thief
    just for the taking

Ridicholas Nicholas

Over Piggledy Pond in back of Beyond
    Flew a truly impossible flock
Of birds on a V from the Alphabet Sea,
    Who settled themselves on the dock.
They clucked and quacked, they quickly unpacked
    And ruffled their feathers for luck.
Then they played a word game with a Loon by the name
    Of Ridicholas Nicholas Duck.

But Ridicholas Nick gave a naughtical flick,
    Swiveling the bill on his head.
And it came as a shock to the flock on the dock
    When that Loonatic Loony bird said,
"You know perfectly well we must first learn to spell.
    I suggest we begin with the dawn."
"T-H-E," quacked the Coot, "D-A-W-N!"
    "Why, you've got it!" cried Nick. "Carry on!"

So they carried on books with blue fishing hooks
    And arranged them in rows on the V.
Then the Swan sang a song that went on for too long,
    And the Goose, oh the Goose,
      Lost her waddle caboose
    Flying back to the Alphabet Sea.

Home Poem
(Or, The Sad Dog Song)

Home of the moth: cloth.
Home of the mole: hole.

Home of the bear: lair.
Home of the ants: pants.

Home of the gnu: zoo.
Home of the flea: me!

A Monumental Bore

The nasty hornet doesn't mind
leaving monuments behind,
and if he lands upon you, kid,
he'll leave a little pyramid.

There Was a Circus

There was the famous dancing bear
Who chased a clown with orange hair.

There were two men whose fingers met
One hundred feet above the net.

There was a walker on a wire,
Three tigers leaped through hoops of fire.

There was the elephant who stood
Upon four boxes made of wood

So that a spotted pig would grunt
And run beneath the elephant.

There was the boy outside the ring
Who thought he had seen *everything*.

Tomcat, Momcat, Babycat, & Me

I like the magic number 3—
   the way it's s'posed to be—
     when 1's the Mom
       and 2's the Tom
         and 3's the kitten, me.

But 1 is growing fat and round,
   2 tiptoes past the door,
     and 3 is me
       and counting
         to the magic
           number 4.

O 2 B A C-Gull

A		
B-gull	The	
Chased	E-gull	The
A	Bit	E-gull
C-gull.	The	Swallowed
An	Flea-gull.	Flea-gull
E-gull	The	And
Chased	B-gull	The
A	Hit	B-gull
Flea.	The	Followed
	Sea.	Me!

Paddy Pork

Paddy Pork
    wakes at nine,
        steps across
            the other swine.

Trots to market,
    buys an ax,
        lugs it home
            in paper sacks.

Paddy heaves-
    ho—high!
        Heavens, how
            the chips fly!

Piggies, hens,
    & roosters stop,
        watching Paddy
            Pork chop.

Summer Fun

Lie beside a caterpillar
Called the woolly bear
Run your finger down along
His hilly brown hair

Take a tiny traveling ant
Set him on your knee
He should reach Mount Elbow
By this afternoon at three

Catch a mighty lightning bug
Put him in a jar
Take him somewhere nice and dark
To see how bright you are

Listen to a cricket play
Her *chicka-chicka* song
Click a clicker
You can *chicka-chicka* play along

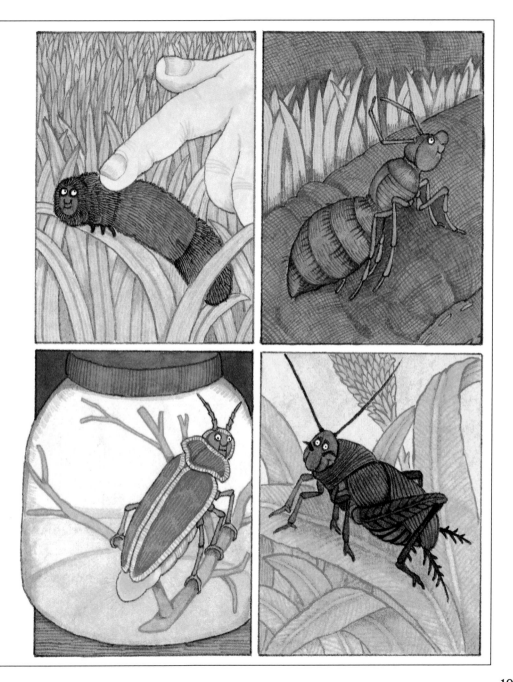

Blue

Fifty tons of muscle
seventy tons of skin & blood & bone
your tongue bigger than an elephant
your glad heart six men could carry
your enormous stone-still eye

& this song halfway to China
from you, Blue, fat with she-calf,
graceful as a cloud sailing down
the long night of the sea

Noisiest of Birds

Noisiest of birds, the magpie sees
To all the latest gossip in the trees,
Forever pestering juncos, jays, and wrens.
To tell the truth, he hasn't many friends.

But if a day has turned from bad to worse,
You wait! The magpie's eager to converse.
And soon enough you'll find a worry gone,
Just listening to him chatter on and on.

Song of the Sunflower

Sky, mother to the Rose
Wind, brother to the Sea
Moon, sister to the Owl
Sun, butter up to me

Sing, Owl, to Sister Moon
Rise, Rose, to Mother Sky
Wave, Sea, to Brother Wind
Set, Sun, on my brown eye

Hawk

Green Emperors of Noon,
　Two lizards sit
　　With one cool tear
　　　In each sunshot eye.

The open earth
　Furnace melts the air.
　　A hawk screams and
　　　Cancels out the sky.

One Fact About

One fact about
the duck-billed plat-
ypus is that
his face is flat.
It doesn't mat-
ter where he's at,
the duck-billed flat-
ypuss goes splat!

Wrong Way Worms

I wiggled wide and waggled
   Over sea-salt sand
With a nifty night crawler
   To the low-tide land.
We slithered down the seashore
   But we had not planned
On this fat and fishy fellow
   With a hook in his hand!

Toothy Crocodile

There was a toothy Crocodile
Who wallowed in the muck,
Counting up how many
Of his many teeth were buck.
One day he'd count to twenty-nine,
The next day fifty-two,
For counting Crocodile teeth
Is difficult to do.
Flamingos, quite by accident,
Would walk across his brain…
But the slightest interruption
Meant he had to start again.

So weeks went by and thus
The counting Crocodile grew thinner,
Because the Alligators ate
The Crocodile's dinner,
While he was much too busy
With a cavern to explore—

"Twenty-seven?"
"Sixty-six?"
"One hundred thirty-four?!"

And as the years slipped quickly by
He shriveled in his skin,
Weeping for the life he'd had
And one that might have been—

"If pink, long-legged birdbrains
Hadn't stumbled in the muck,
I might have figured out," he said,
"How many teeth were buck!"

The Condor Owns a Condo

The Condor owns a condo
   On the cliffs at Malibu.
His cousin has a cabin
   Down the coast in old Peru.

One flies up and one flies down
   Circling through the sky.
They don't have much to say except,

             r u!"   "Good-by
         e   y
       P   y
                      y
    o,   y
   l   y
 l
  e   e
"H   !"

Cricket and Bullfrog

A Cricket once sat down and wept
Because the meadow where he chirped

Had flooded, and the rain had swept
His house away. A Bullfrog burped

An invitation to the Cricket
To climb aboard the Frog Express.

The Cricket handed him his ticket
And thanked him for his kindliness.

They passed a Cow, two Ducks, a Goat,
Three Dragonflies, a swarm of Bees—

At last the bumpy Bullfrog boat
Landed safely overseas.

Hug-Ugh!

Higgledy-piggledy
Boa constrictor's a
Practical joker who
Loves a good tease.

Show him the teeniest
Inch of affection, he'll
Give you a yard and a
Half of a squee-

eeze!   eeze!

Kite-Tails

There was a kat,
who had two kits,
who had two kites with tails.
One kit was called
the Duke of York,
and one the Prince of Wales.

The kittens loved
to chase the kites
until, one windy day,
the Duke looked up
to see the kite
carry the Prince away.

Luna Moth

Out of a windless August night,
A luna moth in ghostly light

Beat softly on my window screen—
Tick-tick-ticking— all silver-green.

She whispered secrets in my ear—
I am but a stranger here.

The stars are scrawled across the sky
By ghostwriters, the Moon and I.

You will not see me here tonight—
I have a thousand stars to write.

Water Safety Tip

Never go wading with minnows.
A minnow, as everyone knows,
    Is an inch of a fellow,
    Who tickles you—*Hel*lo!—
And nibbles the tops of your toes!

Space Needle

The desert cactus, ten feet tall,
Can make a fellow feel small.

The panting lizard licks the air,
Pretending that he doesn't care,

But keeps a cold, suspicious eye
Upon this giant in the sky.

Picture This

Here's my mini-book review
Of *Porcupine Meets Kangaroo!*
Recommended for all ages,
Filled
With
Lovely
Picture
Pages.
Kangaroo to Porcupine,
"Lancelot, will you be mine?"

At the wedding party, she
Hugs him (very carefully)....
Oh, this mystery is splendid—
Musn't tell you how it ended—
But
They
Had
Two
Children.
Who?
Kangapine and Porcupoo.

Digger, Digger

Digger, digger
Underground,
Hole gets bigger,
Hill gets round.
Digger, digger
Down that hole
He'll uncover
Sister Mole.
His toes are shovels,
His nose a scoop,
Up from under the alley—
Oop!

Wolves Waiting

There are the wolves waiting, child.
Here is the lame doe,
Trembling in her small body. The wolves
    know.

There are the bushes walking, child,
Stalking in silvered pairs.
Footfalls no one hears. The doe
    stares.

There is the blizzard coming, child,
Out of the angry skies.
Gray is the color of hope. The doe
    sighs.

Lounge Lizard

Donna Iguana,
Lizard Lady,
Lounges anywhere
It's shady.

Shady or sunny,
I wouldn't wanna
Be Lizard Lady,
Donna Iguana.

A Giraffe by Any Name

Thunderrunner,
Dot-to-dot,
Old Eat-the-sky.

Wooden-knees,
Stick-tree,
Cloud-puller.

Legs-gone-wrong,
Tall-to-heaven,
Singer of small songs.

He whom the sun loves
Loves the sun back.

A Tiptop Tip

Here's a tiptop
tip to travelers
(who may think that
I'm being cynical):
Never get the itch
to hitch a ride on a porcu

p
i
n
n
a
c
l
e
!